The Magic Shark
Learns to Cook

Donivee Martin Laird

Illustrated by
Carol Ann Johnson

3565 Harding Ave.
Honolulu, Hawai'i 96816
Phone: (800) 910-2377
Fax: (808) 732-3627
www.besspress.com

Library of Congress Cataloging-in-Publication Data

Laird, Donivee Martin.
  The magic shark learns to
cook / Donivee Martin Laird ;
illustrated by Carol Ann Johnson.
      p. cm.
  Includes illustrations, glossary.
  ISBN 1-57306-233-2
  1. Sharks - Juvenile fiction.
2. Folklore - Juvenile literature.
3. Cookery - Juvenile literature.
I. Johnson, Carol Ann. II. Title.
PZ7.L158 Mag 2004   398-dc21

Printed in Korea

The characters in this book are from the following titles by Donivee Martin Laird, illustrated by Carol Ann Johnson.

The Three Little Hawaiian Pigs and the Magic Shark

In this adaptation, the three little pigs live in Hawai'i. The Magic Shark (there are no wolves in Hawai'i) has mighty intentions, but is foiled by the pigs and ends up in the local dump.

Keaka and the Liliko'i Vine

This book, based on the story of Jack and the beanstalk, finds Keaka and his mother living in a Hawaiian fishing village. Keaka trades his goat for some liliko'i seeds, and his adventure with the giant and his wife begins.

Wili Wai Kula and the Three Mongooses

Wili Wai Kula is a Goldilocks who lives in Hawai'i. She is told not to go into the forest, but that is exactly what she does. There she finds a house that belongs to a family of mongooses rather than bears.

'Ula Li'i and the Magic Shark

The Magic Shark, who has been rescued from the dump, sees 'Ula Li'i (Little Red Riding Hood) taking a basket of food to her grandmother. The shark tries to outwit the girl and get her basket, but thanks to a brave hanawai man's quick actions, he again ends up in the dump.

Snow White and the Seven Menehune

Lovely Snow White (Hau Kea) lives with seven hard-working menehune until a wicked queen comes along and gives her a poison guava. When the menehune and the Prince of Kaua'i kiss Snow White, she awakens and they all sail off to Kaua'i.

One fine Hawaiian day a rat was strolling through a dump.
He spotted a box of overripe papayas and said, "Mmm—
a papaya smoothie would taste pretty good right now."
"Just what I was thinking," said a voice.

Frosty Papaya Smoothie
Makes 2 ½ cups

1 to 2 C. papaya chunks
1 8-oz. carton vanilla yogurt
2 large scoops vanilla ice cream
1 C. ice cubes
Put everything into a blender, cover, and whirl on
high speed until well mixed—about 30 seconds.

*Turn blender off before sticking
any utensils into it.*

The rat looked to see who was talking and saw a folded, crumpled shark.

"Shark!" he screeched. "Shark!"

He looked closer and said, "Hey, you're the Magic Shark. What happened?"

"I was sort of misbehaving, so a hanawai man tied me up and tossed me in here," answered the shark. "I don't suppose you'd help me get free, would you?"

"And be your dinner? No way!" exclaimed the rat.

"I wouldn't eat you," said the shark. "I tried rat once. It was gross."

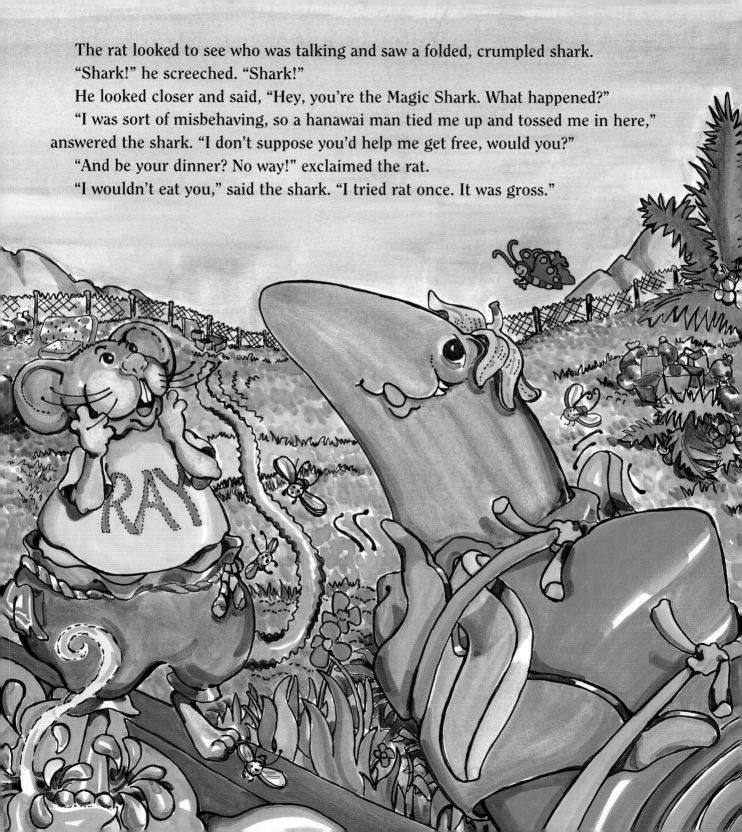

"What will you eat?" asked the rat.

"I'll invite myself to someone's house for something simple, like a kālua turkey quesadilla," answered the shark.

"No one would let you in," said the rat. "You'd better just cook your own quesadilla."

Kālua Turkey Quesadilla
Makes 8 quesadillas

8 flour tortillas
12 oz. kālua turkey
2 C. (8 oz.) shredded cheese
Sour cream

1 ½ C. chopped tomato
½ C. chopped green onion
Butter or margarine
Salsa

Heat a skillet over medium-high heat. Butter one side of a tortilla and place, buttered side down, in the skillet. On one half of the tortilla pile about ¼ C. kālua turkey, ¼ C. cheese, 1 to 3 Tbsp. tomato, and 2 to 3 tsp. green onion. With a spatula or tongs fold the other half over filling. Cook 1 or 2 minutes, until tortilla begins to brown. Carefully flip the tortilla over and cook the other side. Cut into wedges and serve with salsa and sour cream.

Hot skillet—ask for adult help or supervision.

"I don't know how to cook," said the shark.

"Obviously that's something you need to learn," said the rat.

"How can I learn to cook if I am tied up and lying in a dump?" answered the shark.

"So, if you knew how to cook you would just fix your own food and not bother anyone else?" asked the rat.

"Why not? How hard is it to learn to cook?" asked the shark.

"I'm not sure, but I know someone we can ask—my friend Aunty Giant," said the rat. "She's a great cook. She makes an 'ono-licious pineapple-frosted orange cake."

"Let's go see this giant aunty lady and get me some cooking lessons right now," said the shark, enthusiastically.

"Will you promise and cross your heart not to eat me or anyone else if I untie you?" asked the rat.

"I promise, but I can't cross my heart at the moment," answered the shark.

The rat chewed the strings around the shark and set him free.
The shark stretched, groaned loudly, crossed his heart, and smiled.
The rat jumped back. "I'd advise you not to smile too much," he said.
"Oh, sorry," said the shark. His stomach growled.
The rat let out a frightened squeak and said, "Follow me."
He scurried off with the shark huffing and puffing after him.

After a short distance they saw a little girl sitting on her front step eating something out of a bowl.

"What are you eating?" asked the shark.

"Chili Mac," said the little girl, looking up. With a gasp she leaped to her feet and ran into the house, screeching, "Shark! Shark!"

Wili Wai Kula's Chili Mac

Serves 4

2 C. (8 oz.) shredded cheddar cheese
1 8-oz. can vegetable beef soup
8 oz. (about 2 C.) uncooked elbow macaroni
1 4-oz. can diced green chiles, optional*

1 15-oz. can chili
2 C. corn chips, crushed
1 ½ soup cans (12 oz.) water

Set ½ C. cheese and crushed chips aside. Pour everything else into a 2 ½-quart casserole. Stir well and sprinkle with ½ C. cheese and crushed chips. Cover and bake at 350 degrees for 35 to 40 minutes.

Oven will be hot—use pot holders.

*Optional means you don't have to use it.

"Wili Wai Kula," called the rat. "Come back out."

"He will eat me," said Wili Wai Kula.

"He promises he won't. We are going to see Aunty Giant about cooking lessons," said the rat.

"You promise not to eat me?" Wili Wai Kula asked, peeking out the door.

"Yes, I promise," said the shark, "and I cross my heart." He crossed his heart, and his stomach growled.

"Did you hear that? We've got to go," said the rat.

"Wait, I'll go with you," said Wili Wai Kula, bravely.

The rat, shark, and little girl were hurrying along when a voice said, "Shark, what are you doing out of the dump?"

"The hanawai man," yelped the shark, ready to run.

"He promises to behave if he learns how to cook," said Wili Wai Kula.

"Fo' real?" the hanawai man asked.

"Yes, I promise and I cross my heart," said the shark.

"We're on the way to Aunty Giant's house," said the rat.

"That wahine's one good cook," sighed the hanawai man. "I'll go with you."

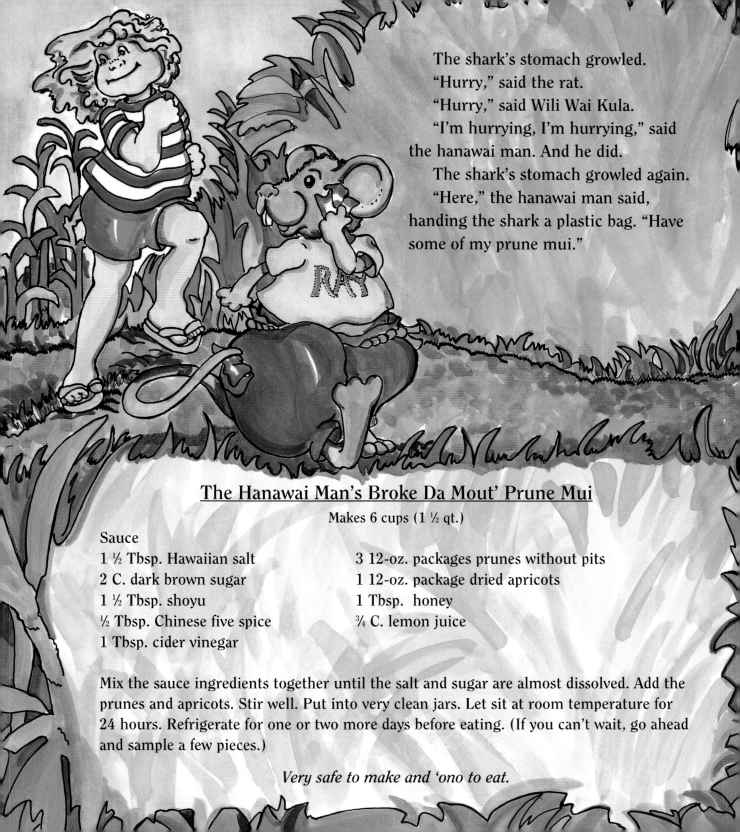

The shark's stomach growled.
"Hurry," said the rat.
"Hurry," said Wili Wai Kula.
"I'm hurrying, I'm hurrying," said the hanawai man. And he did.
The shark's stomach growled again.
"Here," the hanawai man said, handing the shark a plastic bag. "Have some of my prune mui."

The Hanawai Man's Broke Da Mout' Prune Mui

Makes 6 cups (1 ½ qt.)

Sauce
1 ½ Tbsp. Hawaiian salt
2 C. dark brown sugar
1 ½ Tbsp. shoyu
½ Tbsp. Chinese five spice
1 Tbsp. cider vinegar

3 12-oz. packages prunes without pits
1 12-oz. package dried apricots
1 Tbsp. honey
¾ C. lemon juice

Mix the sauce ingredients together until the salt and sugar are almost dissolved. Add the prunes and apricots. Stir well. Put into very clean jars. Let sit at room temperature for 24 hours. Refrigerate for one or two more days before eating. (If you can't wait, go ahead and sample a few pieces.)

Very safe to make and 'ono to eat.

Up, up, up a steep hill they climbed until
they were in front of the biggest house the shark had ever seen.
"Hūi! Aunty Giant," the rat called. "We need some cooking lessons and we need
them right away."

A gigantic woman opened the door. When she saw who was there, she jumped backwards,
screaming, "Shark!" From behind her, two voices cried, "Oh, ah, ouch, Aunty, you're
stepping on me." And "Auwē Aunty, try move your big wāwae."

Two frightened faces peeped around the large skirt. One belonged to Mama Mongoose,
the other to 'Ula Li'i. "Shark!" they screamed, "Shark!"

"Stop!" cried the rat. "He promises not to eat us if he learns how to cook."

The screaming stopped.

"You sure?" asked Aunty Giant.

"You stay promise?" asked Mama Mongoose.

"Yes," said the shark. "I'm sure, I promise, and I cross my heart." He crossed his heart and didn't smile. His stomach growled.

"He's one hungry buggah," said the hanawai man.

"Since you promise and cross your heart, we will teach you how to cook, but you better not try any funny business," said Aunty Giant, "or I'll squash you flat."

"Then I'll crunch you and fold you and tie you up," added the hanawai man.

The shark shuddered at the thought. "Will you teach me to make pineapple-frosted orange cake?" he asked, quickly changing the subject.

"Good idea," said Aunty Giant. "That cake is a big favorite. But before we begin, you all need to wash your hands, paws, and fins."

Mama Mongoose said, "Das right, da hands gotta be clean."

Aunty Giant's Pineapple-Frosted Orange Cake

Makes one rectangle or two round cakes

1 box yellow cake mix   3 eggs
½ cup vegetable oil   1 C. water
1 11-oz. can mandarin oranges, drained

Prepare cake according to directions on the box. Carefully fold in the drained mandarin oranges. Bake at 350 degrees for 35 minutes. Let cake cool.

Frosting
  1 8-oz. container whipped topping   1 3.4-oz. package instant vanilla pudding
  1 8-oz. can crushed pineapple, drained   1 11-oz. can mandarin oranges, drained

Mix the first 3 frosting ingredients together well. When cake is cool, spread with frosting and decorate with mandarin oranges. Chill until ready to serve.

Oven will be hot—use pot holders.

bake: cook food in the oven.

broil: cook by direct heat under a broiler in the top of the oven.

mix: stir foods together so the mixture looks the same all over.

blend: use an electric blender to mix or chop food.

slice: cut across food to make thin pieces.

MEASURING

16 Tbsp. = 1 cup

2 cups = 1 pint

4 cups = 1 quart

8 cups = ½ gallon

16 cups = 1 gallon

When all the hands, paws, and fins were washed, Aunty Giant said, "Next we read our recipe and get out all our ingredients and utensils."

"What was that about my ten window sills?" asked the shark.

No one spoke for a moment.

"Utensils," laughed Wili Wai Kula. "He means utensils."

'Ula Li'i explained, "Utensils are what we cook with, like bowls, pans, spoons, cups—things like that."

"Oh. Then what are ingredaments?" asked the shark.

"In-gre-di-ents," said 'Ula Li'i slowly. "They are the things you mix together to make whatever you are cooking."

"In-gre-di-ents," repeated the shark slowly.

GOOD IDEAS!

BEFORE YOU START TO COOK:
1. Always get permission from an adult.
2. Read the whole recipe.
3. Be sure you have all your ingredients.
4. Get out all needed utensils.
5. Wash your hands in hot, soapy water for at least 20 seconds.
6. Tie back long hair and sleeves.
7. Wear an apron.

Clean as you go. Wipe up spills on the floor so it isn't slippery.

Keep the counters, tables, cutting board, and utensils clean.

Aunty Giant said,

"Your first job is to grease this cake pan."

"No problem," exclaimed the shark, grabbing the pan and rushing out the door. In a few moments he was back. He held up the cake pan. It was smeared with thick, black grease.

"I found just what I needed in the garage," he said. He saw six astonished faces and asked, "Did I do something wrong?"

"The type of grease we use in cooking is butter or cooking oil. That grease is just for cars.

Let's wash these pans and start over," said Aunty Giant kindly.

How to grease a baking pan

You grease a pan to keep food from sticking to it. Check your recipe. It may tell you to grease only the bottom of the pan. Place about a teaspoonful of butter, margarine, or liquid cooking oil in a baking pan. Using a small piece of a paper towel, spread the grease all over the pan until it is evenly coated. You can also use cooking spray. Hold the can about 12 inches from the baking pan and spray until the pan is evenly coated. Do this in the sink or outdoors, as the spray flies all over the place.

The Magic Shark looked at the recipe. "This word says Oz. What does the Wizard have to do with cake?"

"Wizard?" asked Aunty Giant, confused.

"The Wizard from the story about Dorothy," said the shark.

"These are the letters o and z. They are an abbreviation for ounce," explained Aunty Giant.

"What about a sea?" asked the shark. "Isn't a sea pretty big and salty to put in a cake?"

"A sea?" asked 'Ula Li'i.

"Yes, it says a funny number and sea right there in the recipe." The shark pointed.

Aunty Giant explained again, "That is the letter C. It is the abbreviation for cup."

The Magic Shark shook his head. "I'm going to have to learn a whole new language in order to cook."

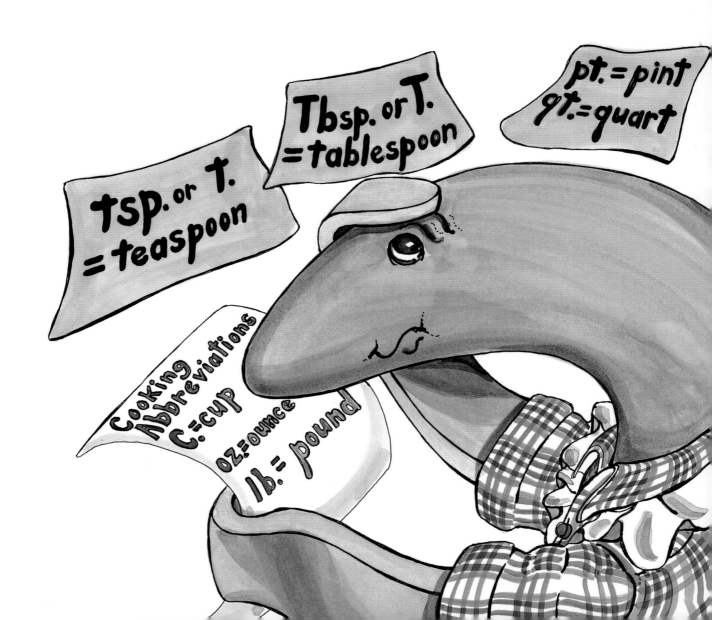

"Shark, please hand me a tablespoon," said 'Ula Li'i.

The Magic Shark muttered, "Table . . . spoon . . . table . . . spoon." He spotted a spoon on the kitchen table and handed it to 'Ula Li'i. He saw her face and asked, "Wrong again?"

She held up four spoons. "These," she said, "are measuring spoons."

"There's that funny-looking number again," said the shark, pointing at a spoon.

"It is a fraction," said 'Ula Li'i.

"So a tablespoon isn't from a table, a teaspoon has nothing to do with tea, and a fraction is a kind of number," thought the shark.

"Dear, please get me a cup of vegetable oil," said Aunty Giant.
The shark filled his favorite cup with oil and tossed in some peas and corn.

"Just as there are special spoons for measuring, there are special cups for measuring," said Aunty Giant, shaking her head and pouring the oil into a measuring cup. (She took the vegetables out first.)

"I get it," exclaimed the shark. "There are special spoons and cups to measure with so you add the same amount of each ingredament every time you cook something. That way the recipe always turns out the same. Right?"

"Right!" said Aunty Giant.

"It's ingredient, not ingredament," said the rat.

"Shark, will you beat these eggs?" asked Aunty Giant.

"Sure, I will beat them. They don't have feet, and I'm a pretty fast runner," said the shark.

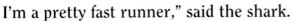

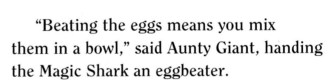

"Beating the eggs means you mix them in a bowl," said Aunty Giant, handing the Magic Shark an eggbeater.

Soon the eggs were clunking around in a bowl.

"You need to crack the eggs open before you beat them," said Aunty Giant.

The shark broke open an egg and dropped it, shell and all, into the bowl.

"You forgot to tell him not to put the shell in the bowl," giggled Wili Wai Kula.

After a few tries the determined shark had beaten the eggs (without any shells). He then added them to the other ingredients and stirred well.

At last Aunty Giant announced, "The cake is ready for the oven."
"It doesn't look like cake," said the shark. "It's gooey."
"It has to bake for thirty-five minutes. Then it will be cake,"
said Aunty Giant.

The shark's stomach growled.
"He's hungry again," said Wili Wai Kula.

"We'll have lunch while the cake bakes," said Aunty Giant. "I made some of Keaka's Magic Bean Salad."

"I'll make tuna sandwiches," said 'Ula Li'i. "Shark, your job is to chop the onion."

The shark rummaged in his backpack and took out a karate uniform. He put it on and held up his hand. "I'm ready to do a chop," he announced.

Everyone began to laugh.

chop: cut food into small pieces on a chopping board. Pieces should be about the size of a pea.

chill: put food in a refrigerator until it is cool.

Aunty Giant calmly explained, "Chop means to cut something into very small pieces. Here is a knife. It is very sharp, so be careful."

"I might cut my fin," said the worried shark.

"A sharp knife, if used correctly, is safest. A dull knife might slip off what you are cutting and cut you," said Aunty Giant.

After a few chops the shark sniffed. "This onion is making me cry and I'm not even sad."

"There is a gas in onions that reacts with the moisture in your eyes to form sulfuric acid," Aunty Giant told the shark. "Tears are the way your eyes wash away the acid."

'Ula Li'i asked, "Aunty, do you think I need to dress the salad some more?"

"Dress it? What does a salad wear?" asked the shark, confused again.

"Salads wear salad dressing," said the rat. He held up a bottle of salad dressing.

"I guess I still have a lot to learn," said the shark.

"You can say that again," said the rat.

"I guess I still have a lot to learn," said the shark.

The rat groaned.

"What is so magic about this salad?" asked the shark, peeking in the bowl. "Will it start growing or something?"

'Ula Li'i laughed. "The magic part is, it is easy to make and 'ono to eat."

She was right. The salad was 'ono and so were the sandwiches.

Keaka's Magic Bean Salad

Serves 6 to 8

3 15-oz. cans of beans—any mixture you like best
(suggestions: kidney beans, garbanzo beans, green or yellow string beans,
black beans, pinto beans)

1 C. cooked brown rice, cooled

⅓ C. chopped yellow, Maui, or green onion   1 C. chopped celery

½ green and ½ red bell pepper, chopped   ½ C. grated carrot

1 C. canned or frozen corn

1 bottle oil-and-vinegar-type salad dressing

Drain and rinse the beans. Combine all the ingredients except the salad dressing in a large bowl. Mix well. Pour on ⅓ to ½ C. salad dressing. Mix again. Eat right away or let sit in the refrigerator for up to 24 hours.

Use knives with help or supervision.

Toasted Tuna Sandwiches by 'Ula Li'i

Makes 2 to 3 open-faced sandwiches

3 to 4 Tbsp. finely chopped onion

1 6-oz. can tuna, very well drained

½ tsp. Italian salad dressing (or more to taste)

3 to 6 Tbsp. mayonnaise

2 to 3 slices bread

2 C. (8 oz.) shredded cheddar cheese or sliced processed American cheese

In a small bowl, mix the onion, tuna, and salad dressing with 3 Tbsp. mayonnaise—more if you like your tuna creamy. Spread a layer of mayonnaise on a piece of bread. Next spread on 3 to 4 Tbsp. of the tuna mixture and top with 3 to 4 Tbsp. grated cheese or 1 cheese slice. Place on a baking sheet, set the oven on broil, and cook until the cheese melts.

Let cool a little. Hot cheese can burn da mout'.

Thirty-five minutes later Aunty Giant showed the shark how to stick a toothpick into the cake to check if it was done.

"See?" she said. "The toothpick doesn't have any of the batter stuck to it, so we know the cake is ready."

"The batter?" shouted the shark. "What is he doing in a hot oven? He'll burn."

"Batter is another name for dough," said Aunty Giant, patiently.

"Dough?" said the astonished shark. "How much is in there? Will we be rich?"

Mama Mongoose said, "Sheese, you one dumb sha'k. Dough is da stuff we stay cooking. Money stay come from one bank."

"He isn't stupid," said Aunty Giant. "This is just all very new to him."

"The cake needs to be cool before we frost it," said 'Ula Li'i.

"Right," said the shark. The next thing everyone knew he was sitting beside the cake in a lounge chair, wearing his jams and sunglasses, reading a magazine, and sipping a drink through a blue straw.

"What are you doing?" asked the rat.

"Being cool with the cake," replied the shark.

"Oh boy," muttered the rat to himself. "It's going to be harder than I expected to teach a shark to cook."

When the cake was finally cool and frosted, the shark ate two pieces and agreed it was the best he had ever tasted.

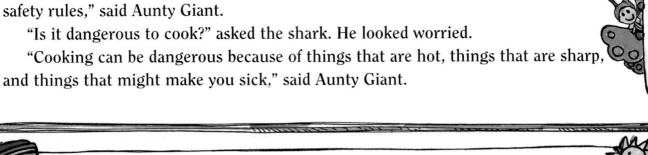

"Before we go any further, you need a list of kitchen and cooking safety rules," said Aunty Giant.

"Is it dangerous to cook?" asked the shark. He looked worried.

"Cooking can be dangerous because of things that are hot, things that are sharp, and things that might make you sick," said Aunty Giant.

KITCHEN SAFETY RULES

A. Always check with an adult before you start a cooking project.
B. Get adult help or supervision when using stoves, ovens, kitchen appliances, or anything sharp, such as knives or open cans.
C. Use pot holders.
D. Wash your hands with hot water and soap before you cook.
E. Wash your cutting board, knives, and hands with hot water and soap after they have touched raw chicken, meat, or eggs.
F. Don't wear long sleeves or baggy clothes that might catch on fire or get stuck in egg beaters. Tie back long hair and wear an apron.
G. Keep handles of pots and pans turned toward the side or back of the stove so you don't bump them.
H. Turn off blenders or electric mixers before you put any utensils in them.
I. Remember, items cooked in a microwave are hot!
J. Be careful taking lids off pots and rice cookers—steam can burn.
K. Wash fresh fruits and vegetables before using them.

"Knives, gas, acid, hot stoves, things that make you sick—cooking is pretty scary sometimes," said the shark.

"So are you," said the rat.

'Ula Li'i handed the shark a list.

"Wow, there is a lot to this cooking stuff," the shark said, wondering if it might not be easier to go back to his old ways. He shook his head.

A promise is a promise. He would learn to cook.

One morning, many cooking lessons later, there was a loud knocking at Aunty Giant's front door.

The shark opened the door and saw two fishermen and the Three Little Hawaiian Pigs. The fishermen were holding a large fishing net.

"There he is!" yelled the First Little Pig.

"Grab him," yelled the Second Little Pig.

The fishermen threw their net over the shark.

"Got him!" they yelled.

"Help!" the shark cried. "Help!"

"What is going on?" asked Aunty Giant in her loud giant voice.

"We heard he was here," said the Third Little Pig. "We've come to save you."

"We're going to make shark steaks out of him," said one of the fishermen.

"No, not steaks!" exclaimed the shark. "Aunty, tell them I've learned to make my own food so I won't bother anyone."

"It's true. He has crossed his heart and promised. I've been teaching him to cook," said Aunty Giant.

"I can prove I've learned to cook," said the shark.
"How?" asked the First Little Pig.
"How?" came an echo from behind Aunty Giant's skirt.
"I'll cook something," answered the shark.
"Oh, oh," said the voices from behind the large skirt.

"Like what?" asked one of the fishermen.

"Well . . . ," said the shark slowly, "how about Hawaiian French Toast?"

The pigs and the two fishermen talked it over.

"We will give you one chance," said the First Little Pig.

"No fooling around and no tricks," said one of the fishermen, "or we will turn you into shark steaks."

The shark was freed from the net. He said, "Thank you," but he knew better than to smile.

Sharky's Hawaiian French Toast

4 servings

2 eggs	Peanut butter
¼ C. milk	¼ C. grated coconut
¼ tsp. cinnamon	8 slices Portuguese sweet bread
¼ tsp. vanilla	Guava jelly
A shake of nutmeg	Maple syrup
2 ½ C. Post Honey Bunches of Oats Cereal, crushed	2 C. sliced fresh pineapple or banana
	8 oz. whipped topping

Preheat oven to 350 degrees. Break eggs into a shallow dish or pie plate. Add milk, cinnamon, vanilla, and nutmeg. Beat with a fork until well mixed. Place crushed cereal in pie plate. Spread a thin layer of peanut butter on four slices of bread and a thin layer of guava jelly on four other slices of bread. Put bread slices together, making four peanut butter and guava jelly sandwiches. Dip each sandwich into egg mixture, then into cereal, turning to coat both sides. Press cereal gently into bread with your hand or a spatula. Place on lightly greased baking sheet. Bake 20 minutes, or until golden brown. Top with maple syrup, fruit, and whipped topping and sprinkle with grated coconut. (For 8 people, double the ingredients.)

Oven will be hot—use pot holders.

In the kitchen, everyone found a place to sit or stand out of the way.

"Here, try these pūpū. I made them myself," said the shark. He passed a crab dip and crackers and barbecue chicken wings with ranch dressing.

Very 'Ono Crab Dip
Makes 2 ½ cups

1 ½ C. imitation crab, shredded
1 C. mayonnaise
1 C. whipped cream cheese
2 tsp. lemon juice (⅛ lemon)
3 Tbsp. green onion, finely chopped
½ C. peeled, grated fresh daikon, optional*
¼ C. Parmesan cheese, optional*
Tabasco, to taste

Combine all of the ingredients in a bowl. Stir gently. Shake in a few drops of Tabasco. (Taste and add more if you like it hotter.) Serve with crackers or chips. This tastes great made with real crab meat.

*Optional means you don't have to use it.

Barbecue Chicken Wings
Pūpū for 5 or 6 people

4 lbs. chicken wings, defrosted and drained
1 18-oz. bottle barbecue sauce
1 16-oz. bottle ranch dressing

Put chicken wings in a large baking pan (9 x 13 inches). If you like your chicken crispier, use two pans so the pieces aren't as close together. Pour the barbecue sauce over the chicken. Mix well. Bake at 400 degrees until the chicken is cooked and turning brown, about 35 minutes. Serve with a ranch dressing dipping sauce.

Oven will be hot—use pot holders.

Then he told his audience, "I have washed my hands and read my recipe. It is time to get out all of my ingredaments, I mean ingredients, and utensils." He counted heads and said, "I'll make twelve servings."

The Magic Shark spread everything he needed on the kitchen counter and took a deep breath.

After the Magic Shark chopped the fruit, he made peanut butter and guava jelly sandwiches. He dipped them in beaten egg (without shells) and milk, rolled them in crushed cereal, placed them on a baking sheet, and put them in the oven. When they were cooked, he proudly served them with maple syrup, fruit, a whipped topping, and grated coconut.

The fishermen, the Three Little Hawaiian Pigs, and the shark's friends unanimously agreed that the Hawaiian French Toast was excellent. They were convinced that the Magic Shark had changed his ways. His lessons were over. Everyone clapped and cheered as Aunty Giant presented him with his own apron and chef's hat.

"Thank you," he said with a huge smile. (No one noticed his teeth.)

The hanawai man offered the Magic Shark back to his ocean home.

"I'll invite you all to dinner soon," called the Magic Shark as the truck drove away.

"I sure hope he learned his lessons well," said the rat, waving good-bye.
"So do we," exclaimed Aunty Giant, ʻUla Liʻi, Mama Mongoose,
Wili Wai Kula, the two fishermen, and the Three Little Hawaiian Pigs
at the same time. "So do we."

GLOSSARY

Auwē! (Hawaiian)—"Oh dear!"

daikon—a root vegetable also known as Japanese radish or Chinese radish. *Daikon* comes from two Japanese words meaning "large" and "root."

hanawai man (Hawaiian)—*Hana* means "work," and *wai* means "water." *Hanawai* means "to irrigate." On sugar plantations in Hawai'i the hanawai men had the job of keeping irrigation ditches operating and free of debris.

hūi (Hawaiian)—a call to get someone's attention.

kālua (Hawaiian)—baked in an imu, or underground oven.

'ono (Hawaiian)—good, delicious, or tasty.

'ōpala (Hawaiian)—trash, garbage.

pūpū (Hawaiian)—hors d'oeuvre, appetizer.

Rei—Hawaiian spelling for the name Ray.
(Note: appears on the rat's shirt)

'Ula Li'i (Hawaiian)—*Li'i* means "little" and *'ula* means "red." 'Ula Li'i is "little red."

wahine (Hawaiian)—woman.

wāwae (Hawaiian)—foot or feet.

Wili Wai Kula (Hawaiian)—*Wili* used here means "twisting lock of hair." *Wai kula* means "gold-colored." Together they mean Goldilocks.

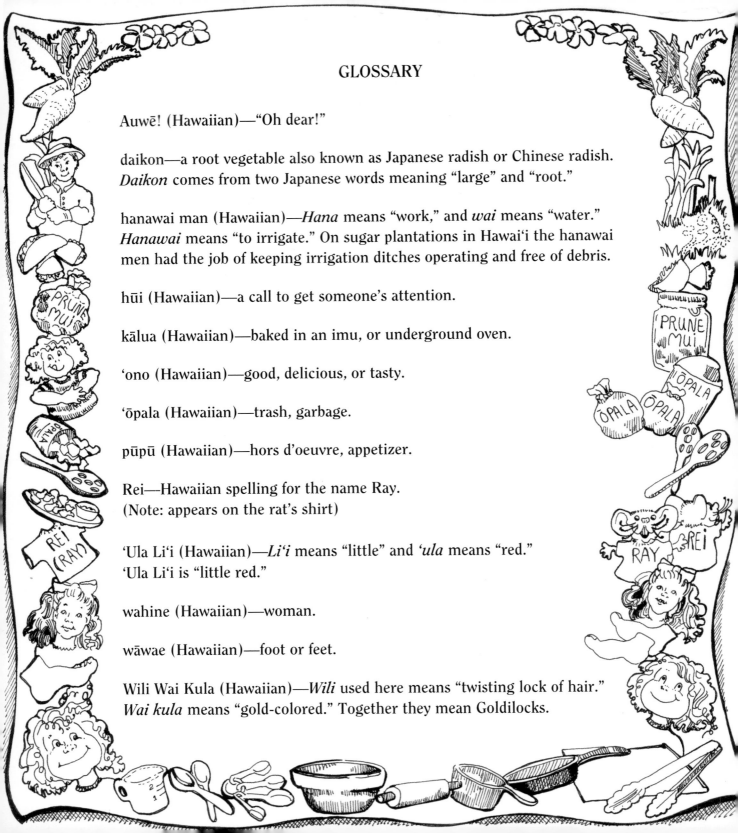